Some Smug Slug

by Pamela Duncan Edwards
illustrated by Henry Cole

HarperCollinsPublishers

P9-DEV-183

The illustrations in this book were painted with acrylic paints and
colored pencils on Arches Hot Press watercolor paper.

S
O
M
E
S
M
U
G
S
L
U
G

Text copyright © 1996 by Pamela Duncan Edwards
Illustrations copyright © 1996 by Henry Cole
Manufactured in China. All rights reserved.
For information address HarperCollins Children's Books,
a division of HarperCollins Publishers,
195 Broadway, New York, NY 10007.

Library of Congress Cataloging-in-Publication Data
Edwards, Pamela.
  Some smug slug / by Pamela Duncan Edwards ; illustrated by Henry
Cole.
      p.   cm.
  Summary: A smug slug that will not listen to the animals around it
comes to an unexpected end.
    ISBN 0-06-024789-4. – ISBN 0-06-024792-4 (lib. bdg.) –
    ISBN 0-06-443502-4 (pbk.)
    [1. Slugs (Mollusks)–Fiction.   2. Animals–Fiction.]   I. Cole, Henry,
ill.   II. Title.
PZ7.E26365So   1996   94-18682
[E]–dc20   CIP
                                                             AC

Typography by Elynn Cohen
❖
15 16 SCP 20 19 18 17 16 15 14 13 12

For dear Peter,
who would have laughed.
—P.D.E.

Stephen—Scooby!
—H.C.

One summer Sunday
while strolling on soil,

with its antennae signaling,
a slug sensed a slope.

Slowly the slug started
up the steep surface,
stringing behind it
scribble sparkling like silk.

"Stop!" screamed a sparrow,
shattering the silence.

9

"Save him!" shrieked a spider,
scurrying down its strand.

11

"Silly," sighed a swallowtail, swooshing through the spice bush.

"Saphead!" snickered a skink
as its sapphire tail swished.

With a shrug of its shoulders, on the slug sauntered. With a swagger it slithered up, up the slant.

"Show-off," scolded a squirrel, storing nuts for the season.

"So sad," squealed a stink bug, shivering on a stem.

For one single second
in a sunbeam it slumbered;
its sleek skin was soft like
shantung.

19

Seldom swerving or straggling
or swaying or skewing,

the smug slug shambled on.

Struggling up to the summit,
the slimy slug smiled
a self-satisfied smile.

In spite of sinister signs,
it showed no suspicion,

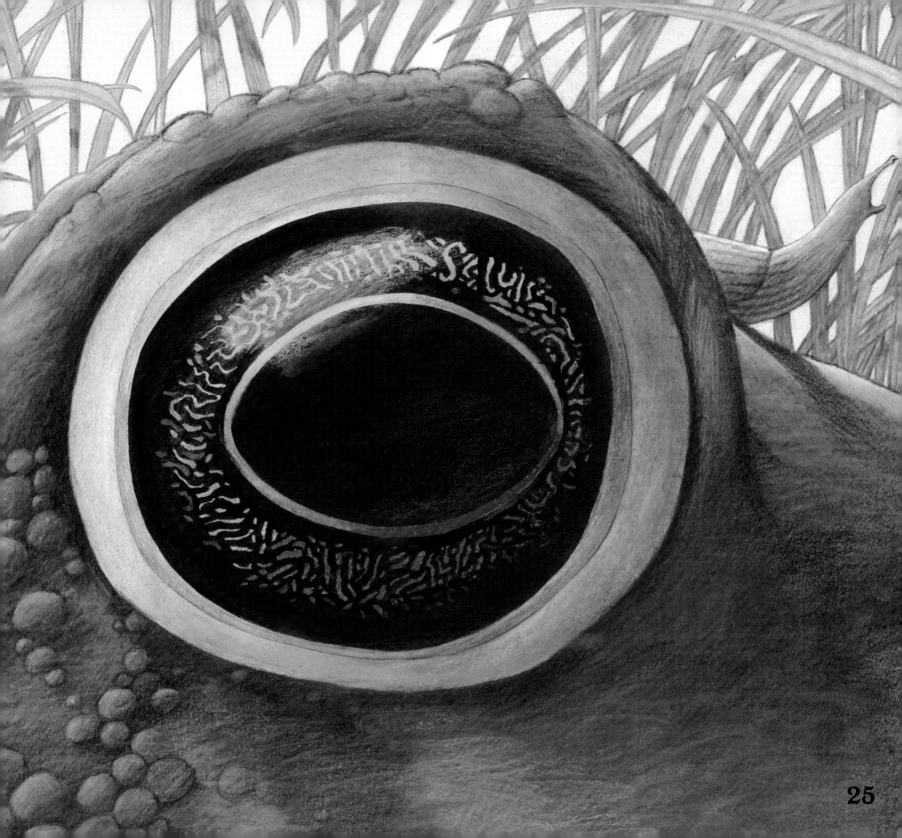

until something shifted,
and shuddered and shook.

That sly, slippery slope
was simply a sham.

Such a shock, such a shame.

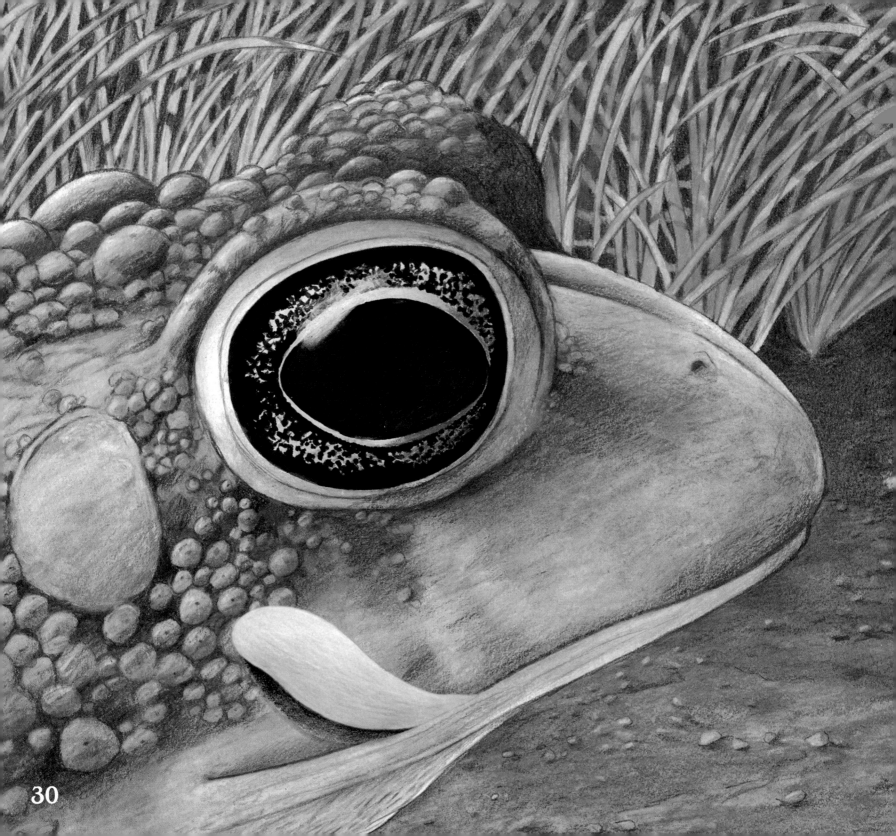

Such a succulent slug!

Somewhere in this story,
did you see a skunk, a snake, a salamander,
and two snails spying on the slug?

Also hidden in each picture is an "S" shape.
Can you spot it?